W9-DHF-408

Family Story Collection

⸎

Don't Judge a Book
by Its Cover

STORIES ABOUT FAIRNESS AND GOOD JUDGMENT

⸎

Book Six

INCLUDING CHARACTERS FROM YOUR FAVORITE · PIXAR FILMS

Printed in China
First Edition
1 3 5 7 9 10 8 6 4 2

ISBN 0-7868-3530-3

For more Disney Press fun, visit www.disneybooks.com

Book Six

———— ⦿⦿⦿ ————

Don't Judge a Book by Its Cover

———— ⦿⦿⦿ ————

STORIES ABOUT FAIRNESS AND GOOD JUDGMENT

Introduction

Children often organize their world into categories. One of the ways they classify people is through others' similarities to and differences from themselves. Learning to accept, and even embrace, differences, brings children to a greater understanding of the world around them.

In "The Odd Couple," Boo is scared of monsters, while Sulley is frightened of human children. It is only when they both can overlook the stereotypes they were taught that they discover they are destined to be friends. Scamp, in "The Other Side," longs for the wild life, while Angel wishes she had a stable home and a loving family. By seeing his world through Angel's eyes, Scamp begins to realize just how fortunate he is.

The Odd Couple

from *Monsters, Inc.*

Just because something is different doesn't mean it's scary.

All over the world, bedtime follows the same pattern.

"Good night," a parent says. "Good night," a child replies.

The lights are turned off, and the parent leaves. The child looks around, and suddenly the familiar bedroom is filled with scary shapes and shadows. Is that something moving over there? What is that sound coming from under the bed? Could the closet door really be creaking open?

"*Aaaaaaaah!*" the child screams as a monster leaps out and roars. The monster is so strange, so terrifying, that the child's only response is to scream and hide. If the child only knew that the monster was actually as scared of him as he is of the monster. . . .

Back in Monstropolis, only the finest monsters were chosen for the risky job of collecting screams.

Once in a while, a monster slipped up, and a human item—a stray sock or toy—made its way into Monstropolis. When that happened, everyone rushed to decontaminate the entire area—including the monster itself.

One day, the unthinkable happened—
a human child made her way into
Monstropolis! It occurred when a monster
named Sulley encountered a child who
wasn't afraid of him. In fact, she followed
Sulley back through the door between their
two worlds. When Sulley realized what had
happened, he was terrified. A child on the
loose would cause chaos in Monstropolis!

It didn't take long for Sulley to learn
that the little girl wasn't as scary as he had
thought. In fact, she was sort of . . . cute and
lovable. He even gave her a name—Boo.
Although they were different, Sulley and Boo
became friends.

But one day, Boo saw a different side of
Sulley. His boss asked him to demonstrate

how to scare children. Sulley entered a fake bedroom and gave a terrifying *ROARRRR!*

He didn't realize that Boo was watching him. She whimpered with fear. Maybe Sulley wasn't so nice after all! He was so scary, so different. . . .

Sulley reassured her. "Boo, it's just me!" he said gently. His words comforted her, and Boo was no longer afraid. Even though he roared like a monster, Sulley was still her friend.

And he proved it by working with his best friend, Mike, to make sure Boo made it home safely. They had quite an adventure, but after a lot of hard work, they were able to get Boo home.

Once back in Boo's bedroom, Sulley tucked her into bed with her favorite teddy bear. "Nothing's going to scare you anymore," he said.

Sulley was sad to say good-bye to his friend, but happy he had learned that children were not scary after all. And Boo learned that a monster could be a loyal friend.

The Other Side

from *Lady and the Tramp II: Scamp's Adventure*

Sometimes you have to leave to appreciate what you've left behind.

Through the fence in his backyard, Scamp spied a group of wild dogs tussling with the dogcatcher. Now *that* was the life for him!

Scamp didn't think he belonged in a house with a family. He was a wild dog at heart, and he daydreamed about life on the other side of the fence. No baths, no leash, no rules. What could be better?

That night, Scamp ran away. Soon after, he met Angel, a pretty little stray dog. The two became fast friends. Angel took Scamp back to the junkyard to meet the other wild dogs.

The Junkyard Dogs were a rough crowd, and they didn't take to strangers quickly. "Hey, collar boy! How's life on the end of a chain?" they jeered at Scamp.

"I've had enough of the house-dog life!" Scamp assured them. "I want to be free like you guys!"

The next night, Angel and Scamp took a walk along the train tracks together. "What are you doing out here?" Angel asked. "Don't you have a nice family back home?"

Scamp explained that having a family meant taking baths, eating out of bowls, and sleeping in a bed. Who would want that?

Angel confessed that she would. She longed to be adopted. "The Junkyard Dogs aren't much of a family," she said sadly. "But what choice do I have?"

"What more do you need?" Scamp asked. He didn't see that the wild life had its downside, too.

Just then, a train came barreling down the tracks behind them.

"Run!" yelled Angel.

Scamp raced ahead. This was just the kind of excitement he had been looking for! But as he neared safety, his paw got stuck in the tracks. Angel ran back for him, and seconds before the train passed over them, they crashed through the railroad ties into the river below.

They finally found each other on the riverbank. The world away from home was more dangerous than Scamp had imagined. He was beginning to realize that the junkyard life wasn't all fun and games.

They continued to walk, and after a little while, they ended up in Scamp's old neighborhood. He decided to take a peek in his family's window. Scamp was surprised to see that everyone looked so sad. They had spent the whole day searching for him.

"Gosh, I didn't think they'd miss me that much," said Scamp, feeling guilty.

"I can't believe you'd run away from a home like this," said Angel in disbelief. "I'd give anything to have what you have."

Maybe Angel had a point, thought Scamp. He had never stopped to think about what he *did* have. He was usually too busy thinking about what he *didn't* have. Scamp was beginning to think that his old life wasn't so bad, after all.